SPIES

SPY [GEAR]

by MICHAEL MARTIN

Consultant:
Jan Goldman, EdD
Founding Board Member
International Intelligence Ethics Association
Washington, D.C.

Mankato, Minnesota

Edge Books are published by Capstone Press,
151 Good Counsel Drive, P.O. Box 669, Mankato, Minnesota 56002.
www.capstonepress.com

Printed in the United States of America

Library of Congress Cataloging-in-Publication Data
Martin, Michael, 1948–
Spy gear / by Michael Martin.
p. cm. — (Edge Books. Spies)
Summary: "Discusses the machines, weapons, and other equipment used by spies as they gather intelligence" — Provided by publisher.
Includes bibliographical references and index.
ISBN-13: 978-1-4296-1304-0
ISBN-10: 1-4296-1304-1
1. Espionage — Equipment and supplies — Juvenile literature. I. Title. II. Series
UB270.5.M365 2008
327.12028'4 — dc22 2007033574

Editorial Credits
Abby Czeskleba and Angie Kaelberer, editors; Bob Lentz, book designer; Jo Miller, photo researcher

Photo Credits
Alamy/Charlie Schuck, 4 (woman); Frank Chmura, 27; Popperfoto, 18 (back)
AP Images/CIA, 18 (front); Heribert Proepper, 8; RTR-Russian Television Channel, 14
Corbis/Bettmann, 12 (left); Jeffrey L. Rotman, 17, 24, 25; zefa/Tim McConville, cover
Getty Images Inc./Mark Wilson, 9 (umbrella); Stone/Paul Edmondson, 23; Time Life Pictures/William Foley, 12 (right)
The Image Works/Syracruse Newspapers, 13
iStockphoto/Vadim Kozlovsky, 22
Shutterstock/Adam J. Sablich, 10 (left); Aga, 9 (grid); Andy Piatt, 3; Black Ink Designers, Corp., 4 (computer chip), 30; David Gordon, 10 (right); Dejan Lazarevic, 9 (audio signal); Feng Yu, 5; Glenn Walker, 7 (left); John Bailey, 7 (middle); kash76, 7 (right); Kevin L. Chesson, 28
ullstein bild/The Granger Collection, New York, 20

1 2 3 4 5 6 13 12 11 10 09 08

TABLE OF CONTENTS

CHAPTER 1

THE RIGHT TOOL FOR THE JOB

LEARN ABOUT:

- Secret devices
- Spy disguises
- Communication

Today's spies use their eyes, ears, and gear to collect information.

Spies can be anywhere. They can be sitting next to you on the bus. They can even be in your family. Spies don't always wear a hat and trench coat like they do in movies. Spies can make themselves look like anyone.

Hundreds of years ago, spies had very little gear. They used their eyes and ears. For example, a spy would hide and count the number of enemy soldiers as they passed. Then the spy would pass the information to an army general. The general would use the spy's information to decide if the army should attack.

Today's spies use lots of advanced gear, but they must be careful. Spies never know who is watching or listening. Government officials must protect information so it doesn't fall into the wrong hands. Important **documents** are kept in guarded rooms or locked in a safe. New weapons are kept on military bases. Leaders talk about their plans in safe locations.

document

a piece of paper that contains important information

Finding out what enemies are doing is important. That is why the Central Intelligence Agency (CIA) exists. One of the CIA's jobs is to gather intelligence for the United States. CIA spies use some of the coolest and most current spy gear.

SECRET DEVICES AND DISGUISES

Intelligence agencies give spies secret **devices** to help spies do their jobs. Many of these devices are so small that people don't notice them.

Spies also use disguises to do their jobs. A different appearance can help keep spies safe. Spies may put on or change their disguises if they think enemies are following them. A disguise may help a spy escape a dangerous setting.

device

a piece of equipment that does a particular job

The CIA spends thousands of dollars developing good disguises. A good disguise helps a spy blend into the surroundings.

Spies use makeup as a part of their disguises. Makeup allows spies to look younger or older. They might put cotton balls inside their cheeks to change the appearance of their face. Or they might use a lifelike mask that hides their face. Special shoes can make spies look taller or cause them to walk with a limp. With a good disguise, a young spy can look like an elderly gentleman.

COMMUNICATION AND DEFENSE

Spies use secret codes, special radios, and other devices to send and receive secret messages.

Spies sometimes carry weapons to protect themselves. Weapons can be hidden or disguised as something else.

The Soviet Union's intelligence agency, the KGB, disguised a weapon as an umbrella to kill Georgi Markov in 1978. Markov was a Bulgarian. He worked as a radio announcer and complained about the Bulgarian government on the air. He complained because he did not agree with the government. Bulgarian leaders wanted him dead.

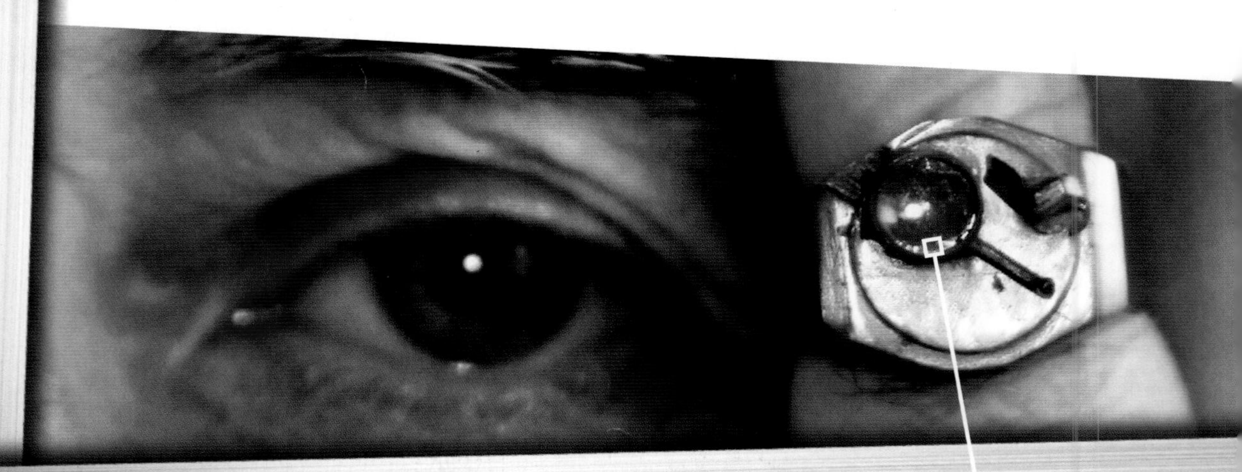

Spies use special devices like this ring camera to secretly take pictures.

A look-alike of the umbrella that killed Georgi Markov is on display at the International Spy Museum in Washington, D.C.

The KGB put a pellet full of poison in the tip of the umbrella. A Bulgarian secret service agent then poked Markov with the umbrella. Markov became sick and died a few days later.

The KGB ended in 1991 when the Soviet Union divided into different republics. Today, the largest former Soviet republic is Russia. The FSB is Russia's intelligence agency.

SPY FACT

KGB spies used a wristwatch radio that displayed messages on a screen. A small receiver hidden in the spy's clothing vibrated when there was a message.

[CHAPTER 2]

COLLECTING INFORMATION

LEARN ABOUT:

- > Breaking and entering
- > Disguising spy gear
- > Hidden cameras

Spies use lock pick tools to break into rooms.

Good spies have the skill of burglars, but it is not money or jewels that spies are after. Instead, spies want information. Spies often need to break into locked rooms or buildings to get information.

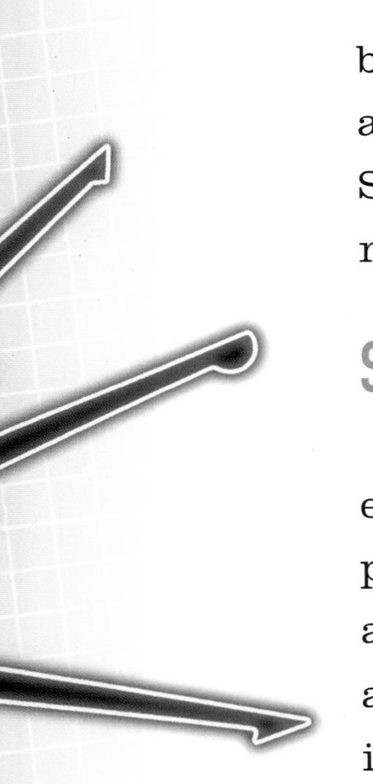

SNEAKING IN AND OUT

A spy may carry what looks like an eyeglasses case. The case holds tools to pick locks. There are very few locks that a spy cannot open. Sometimes spies use a lockpick gun to unlock doors. It goes into the keyhole of a door handle and breaks open the lock.

Spies must act quickly and carefully once inside a building or a locked room. Spies don't usually steal documents because it is better to photograph, copy, or memorize information. That way, no one will know the documents have been stolen.

HIDDEN CAMERAS AND BUGS

Spies use hidden cameras to take pictures of people, places, and documents. A spy who needs information about a new battleship may take a picture of the ship with a hidden camera. Spies can hide cameras in watches or behind shirt buttonholes and belt buckles.

A bug was sewn into a rug with wires that look like thread. Another bug was found in an electrical receptacle outlet.

SPY FILES: SNEAKING A PEEK

Sometimes spies need to know what is in a room before they break into it. They use a tool called a fiberscope to see what is inside a room. A fiberscope can go under doors or through a keyhole. Sometimes a small hole can be drilled in a wall. The fiberscope is pushed through the hole. The spy can then look around without going into the room. Doctors also use fiberscopes, but for a different reason. They use fiberscopes to see inside the human body.

Spies also gather information with secret recording devices. A spy might hide a microphone in a pen, watch, or necktie to record an important meeting. Spies who break into buildings may leave listening devices called **bugs**. Bugs are so tiny that they can be hidden almost anywhere. Bugs have been found inside phones, electrical receptacle outlets, and furniture. One bug was designed to look like a lump of chewing gum stuck under the table.

bug

a hidden recording device

[CHAPTER 3]

SENDING MESSAGES

LEARN ABOUT:

- Dead drops
- Spy codes
- Microdots

In 2006, Russian television reported that British spies used this fake rock as a dead drop.

Gathering intelligence isn't the only tricky part of being a spy. Spies also have to secretly pass information to their case officers. A case officer is a spy's boss. The case officer gives instructions and gear to the spy. Spies and case officers need safe ways to communicate.

DEAD DROPS

Spies try not to be seen with each other because it is dangerous. Instead, they often leave messages at a **dead drop**. A dead drop can be a hole in a tree trunk or a brick wall. Spies can also use hollow spikes to leave messages for each other. The spikes are usually less than 8 inches (20 centimeters) long. Messages or small items are put inside the spikes. Then the spike is placed in the ground. An empty bottle can show the spy who picks up the information where to look.

dead drop

a secret location where spies can leave messages and gear for their case officer or another spy

A spike is not the only special container spies use for dead drops. A magnetic container can be placed under a metal park bench or attached to another metal item. A heavy waterproof pouch can be placed under a rock in a small stream.

SENDING MESSAGES

Getting secret information out of another country is dangerous. Spies who are caught with secret information may be killed. To avoid being caught, spies send messages to each other with hidden radio **transmitters**. During World War II (1939–1945), spies used transmitters disguised as suitcases. Today, spies may use a tiny transmitter or a cell phone that sends messages through radio signals.

transmitter

a device that sends out radio or television signals

A transmitter can be hidden on the back of a tie.

SPY FACT

In Europe, spies used dead rats as dead drops. The spies had to stop using the rats because hungry cats kept eating the secret messages.

Messages are usually sent in secret code. If an enemy finds a coded message, it will be difficult to understand. Messages may be written on paper with invisible ink. Words appear after chemicals are used on the paper. Spies can also print a picture over the message. Chemicals make the picture disappear so spies can read the message.

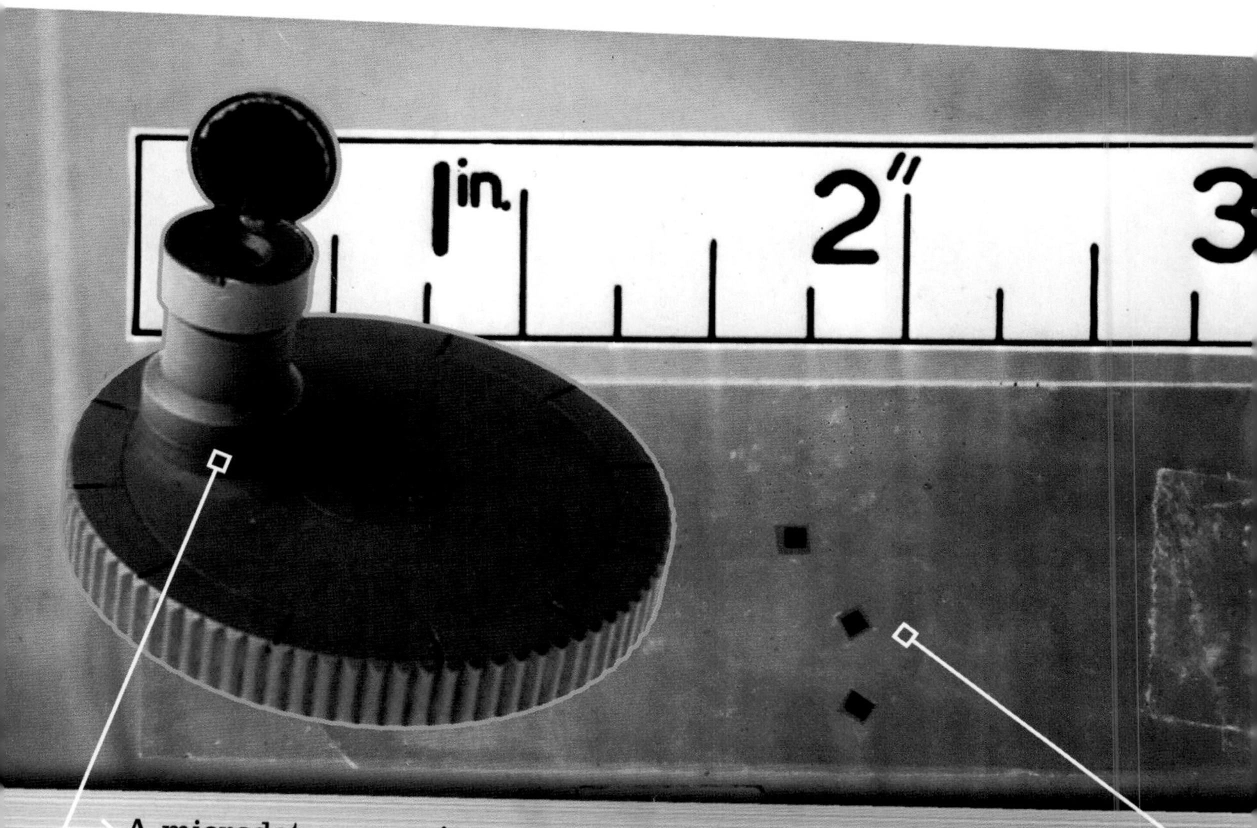

A microdot camera is used to make microdots. Three microdots are magnified one-and-a-half times in this photo.

SPY FILES: REVEALING THE SECRET

One-time pads are notebooks that spies use to code their messages. Some pads are as small as postage stamps. Each pad has a key that tells the reader what the code means. Only two copies of the key are made. The spy has the first copy and the receiver has the second copy. The spy and receiver are the only people who know what the code means. After the message is read, the spy and receiver destroy the message. One-time pads are still being used in some countries, but not in the United States.

Microdots are a clever way to send information. Spies use a microdot camera to take a picture of top-secret information. The camera shrinks the information to the size of a dot. These tiny dots are read with a magnifying lens. The microdots can be hidden almost anywhere. They have been found on coins and rings. Spies can also use a postcard slitter to make a small cut in a postcard. The spy then places a microdot inside the cut and sends the postcard through the mail.

microdot

a small dot that contains a secret message

CHAPTER 4

WEAPONS

LEARN ABOUT:

- Sabotage
- Assassinations
- Future spy gear

During World War II, soldiers did searches to make sure people weren't spies on sabotage missions.

Imagine how scary **sabotage** missions are for spies. These spies must purposely destroy an enemy's property. Spies may also try to ruin an enemy's plans as part of the sabotage mission. If spies are caught, they could be killed. Spies carry special weapons on sabotage missions to protect themselves.

During World War II, British spies carried bombs that looked like coal. They secretly placed these bombs in piles of coal. When the bombs were put into a furnace or engine, they exploded and caused great damage.

GUNS

Spies often have silencers on their guns. A silencer fits on the end of a gun. When the gun fires, it makes very little sound because of the silencer. Some silencers look like flashlights.

sabotage

damage or destruction of property that is done on purpose

No matter how large the silencer, guns still make noise. During World War II, spy agencies experimented with other kinds of silenced weapons. In the 1970s, the British developed a powerful steel crossbow that shot a knife blade or steel bolt. Today, gun silencers are common because they are easier to use than other silenced weapons.

> Spies may use a silencer (top), automatic handgun (middle), and lantern (bottom).

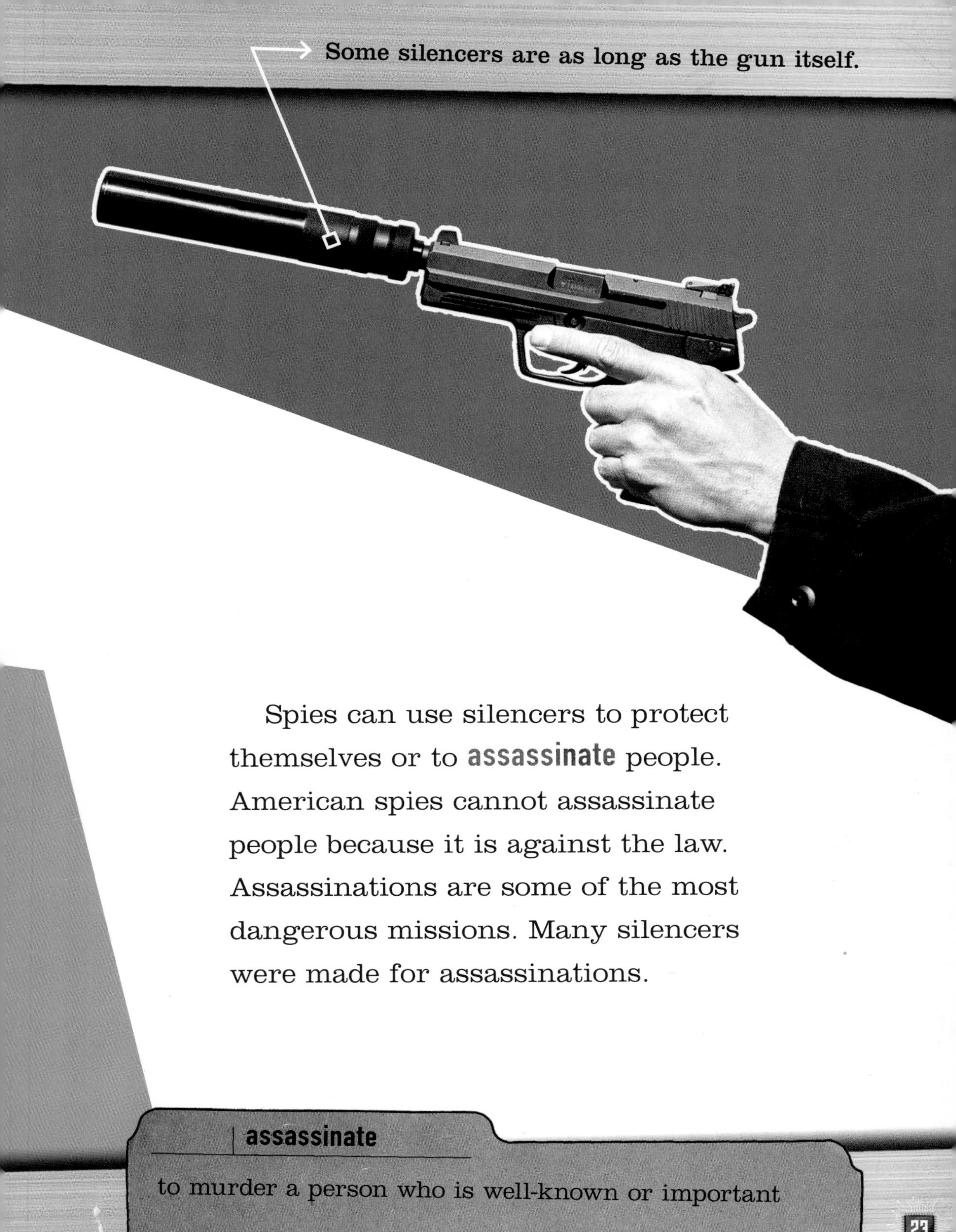
Some silencers are as long as the gun itself.

Spies can use silencers to protect themselves or to **assassinate** people. American spies cannot assassinate people because it is against the law. Assassinations are some of the most dangerous missions. Many silencers were made for assassinations.

assassinate

to murder a person who is well-known or important

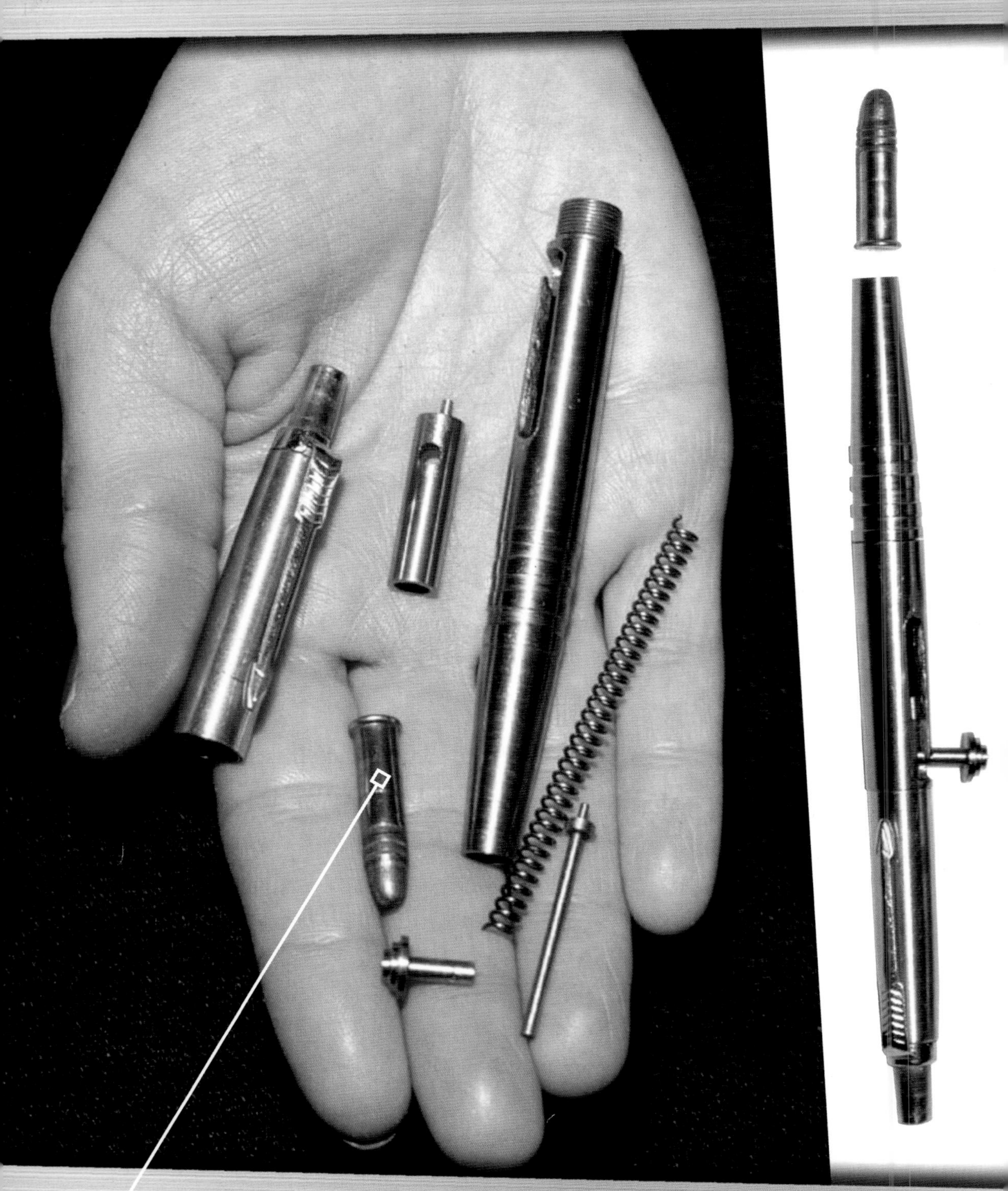

Spies use bullet pens because they are small and easy to hide.

Guns that fire only one bullet can be cleverly disguised as pens, pencils, or flashlights. Spies use these guns in dangerous situations.

The KGB used a gun that looked like a small metal pipe. It was a single-shot gun with a silencer. The gun could be carried in a rolled-up newspaper. On a noisy city street or subway, no one could hear the shot.

UNIQUE WEAPONS

The KGB used unusual methods for assassinations. They developed a poison-tipped umbrella. They made a cane and wallet that shot poison at victims.

Only in the world of spies could an umbrella, a cane, and a wallet be considered deadly weapons.

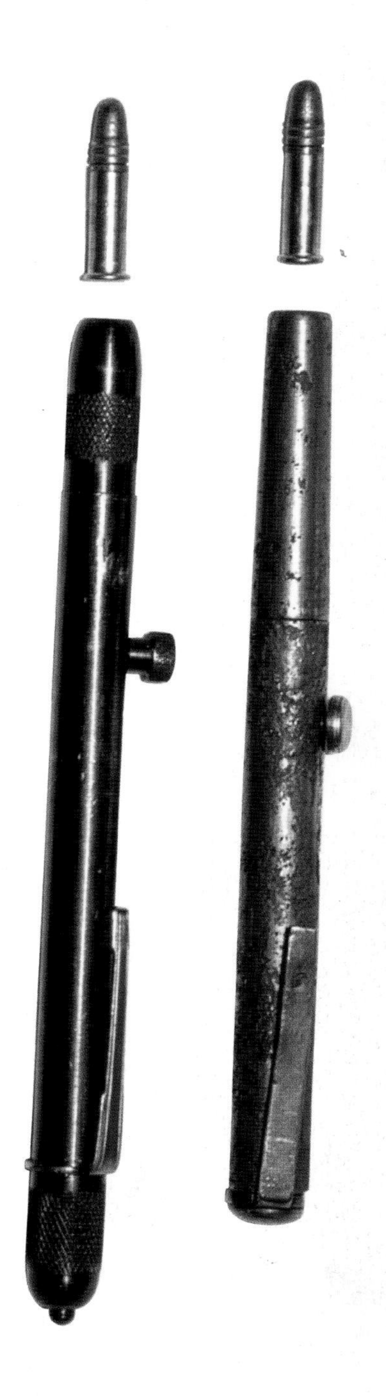

The KGB also used gas guns. The guns fired poisonous gas into a person's face and killed the victim almost instantly. The victim appeared to have died of a heart attack.

SPY GEAR OF THE FUTURE

Over the years, spy gear has become smaller. But new gear does not always have to be small for it to be useful. In 2006, the U.S. government bought two new kinds of spy gear. The first was a foreign language program for computers. The program is called English Now. It can change a foreign language into English. Spies can read the messages even if they can't speak the foreign language.

> Spies use computer programs like English Now
to read messages written in foreign languages.

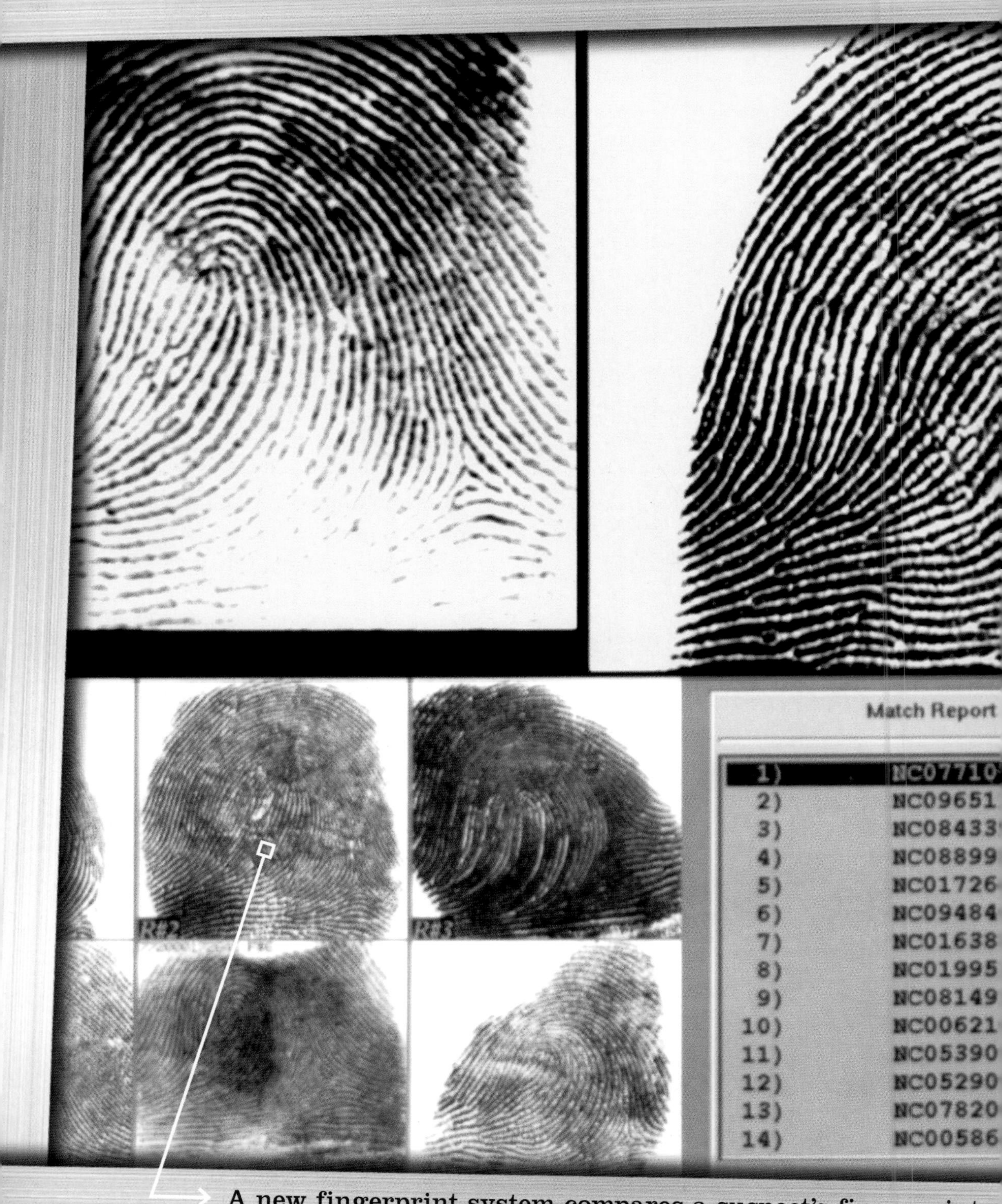

A new fingerprint system compares a suspect's fingerprints with the fingerprints of criminals from around the world.

The U.S. government also bought a fingerprint system. A computer can check if a **suspect's** fingerprints match the fingerprint records of criminals. It only takes the system two minutes to find out the suspect's fingerprint information. The system is able to check the fingerprints of suspects from all over the world. Spies can use the fingerprint system to see if a person has a criminal record.

As new technology develops, it will become easier for spies to do their jobs. Just imagine what spy gear will be developed next!

suspect

someone who may be responsible for a crime

GLOSSARY

assassinate (us-SASS-uh-nate) — to murder a person who is well-known or important

bug (BUHG) — a hidden recording device

dead drop (DED DROP) — a secret location where spies can leave messages and gear for their case officer or another spy

device (di-VISSE) — a piece of equipment that does a particular job

document (DAHK-yuh-muhnt) — a piece of paper that contains important information

intelligence (in-TEL-uh-jenss) — sensitive information collected or analyzed by spies

microdot (MYE-kroh-dot) — a small dot that contains a secret message

sabotage (SAB-uh-tahzh) — damage or destruction of property that is done on purpose

suspect (SUHSS-spekt) — someone who may be responsible for a crime

transmitter (transs-MIT-uhr) — a device that sends out radio or television signals

READ MORE

Fridell, Ron. *Spy Technology.* Cool Science. Minneapolis: Lerner, 2007.

Rollins, Barbara B., and Michael Dahl. *Fingerprint Evidence.* Forensics Crime Solvers. Mankato, Minn.: Capstone Press, 2004.

Walker, Kate, and Elaine Argaet. *Spies and Their Gadgets.* Spies and Spying. North Mankato, Minn.: Smart Apple Media, 2003.

INTERNET SITES

FactHound offers a safe, fun way to find Internet sites related to this book. All of the sites on FactHound have been researched by our staff.

WWW.FACTHOUND.COM®

Here's how:

1. Visit *www.facthound.com*
2. Choose your grade level.
3. Type in this book ID **1429613041** for age-appropriate sites. You may also browse subjects by clicking on letters, or by clicking on pictures and words.
4. Click on the **Fetch It** button.

FactHound will fetch the best sites for you!

INDEX